The Geography

Cath Barton

To Margaret

Cath x

ARROYO SECO PRESS

Logo by Morgan G Robles
morganrobles.carbonmade.com

Arroyo Seco Press

www.arroyosecopress.org

Cover art: cover image by Mari-Anne Gibson from Pixabay

ISBN: 979-8-9895659-0-0

for all who love walking the hills

Contents

Author's note:

This is a work of fiction. It is set in a real town, in (for the most part) real locations; there are references to some real people and some of the events described really happened, but the characters in the story—Megan, her family and the people she meets in the town—are all creatures of my imagination.

The town

Abergavenny has seven hills, like Rome. I like to tell people that. And it is true. Sugar Loaf, Rholben, Deri, Llanwenarth Breast, Skirrid Fawr, Skirrid Fach, and last but not least Blorenge, the only word to rhyme with orange. And, according to local legend, full of water. Stand on the hummocky northern edge of it and look at the town laid out below you. See the little green turret on top of the Town Hall building, which is also the Theatre, which is also the Market. Westwards from there the bulk of the Roman Catholic church, the chimney of the modern hospital and, on the eastern edge of town, the buildings of Pen-y-Fal, the asylum for the unfortunate now turned into housing for the very-much-more-than-usually fortunate. Northwards the streets of the Mardy stretch up under the Deri, the foothill of Sugar Loaf named for its oak trees. Nowadays the roofs of the houses on the Mardy carry rows of solar panels. For the sun does shine in Wales, contrary to what some people will tell you.

When I, Megan Louise Pritchard, first came to Abergavenny it was to go up the Blorenge. I was on a geography field trip from school. If we had gone as far as that view over the town the landmarks would have been the same as now, though without the solar panels. But I don't think we did. All I remember—helped by a bleached-out photograph—is sitting on the rocks at the summit with nuns in habits, eating hard-boiled eggs. We must have set off from the car park named after Foxhunter, the champion show-jumper buried up there on the mountain only a few years before that school visit. There's a good path to the rocks from there, so it's not as surprising as you might think that nuns in habits could manage the walk.

Decades later I'm walking with friends over that same hill when I get a phone call. It is from a paramedic who tells me his name is Adam and that he has been called to Gwladys Pritchard's flat in Abergavenny. Gwladys is my mum. Adam is totally professional and very kind. In answer to his question, I say no, this time my mum should not go to hospital. I ask him if she's going to die and he says yes, but he can't say when, it could be in minutes or hours. I set off down the mountain. Walking is a good time for thinking, thinking about Mum, and about me, and about the geography of this place where we both live.

Beatlemania

When I was thirteen the Beatles were well on their way to becoming famous. But not so famous that they weren't still doing gigs wherever they could get them. On 22 June 1963 they were booked to play Abergavenny Town Hall and my cousin Lili had a ticket. Lili lived in a council house with her mum, Bronwen, who was my mum's sister and had married beneath her, according to Mum. I was only too well aware, even then, that my mum was a terrible snob.

It was a Saturday. Lili told me that she and her friends spent the morning in the Wimpy in Frogmore Street eyeing up the local talent as the lads walked up and down the street, and the afternoon getting ready for their Big Night Out. Lili was fifteen and apprenticed as a hairdresser, so she did all the girls' hair. She did the best beehives, everyone said so, apparently. I thought she was very bold and very grown up.

The local paper reported that there were 600 people at the gig, and that John Lennon was flown into Pen-y-Pound football ground by helicopter as he'd been on Juke Box Jury earlier in the evening.

'I never seen so many people in one place before, Megan,' Lili said when she told me the story. 'And the noise!'

'Did you scream, Lili?'

'Of course! Everyone did—you would have!'

'And did girls, you know, did they?'

'I couldn't say, Megan,' said my cousin, suddenly all coy.

Lili and Bronwen used to come over to where we lived in Beaconsfield every Christmas. Lili's dad Ron never came, and we never went to Wales. I tried asking Mum why, but she'd always change the subject. I always thought it was something to do with Lili's dad not being good enough for Mum. Though goodness knows she was one to talk, what with my dad having done a bunk when I was three. Good riddance as far as I was concerned, though Mum for some inexplicable reason wouldn't have a word said against him.

Lili and her friends had their picture taken for the local paper on the night of the Beatles' gig, she said, but they never printed it, which was, as Lili said, a crying shame, because she reckoned she could have sold it for a lot of money. I wondered why she hadn't got an autograph.

That would definitely have made her money. The trouble was that money ran through Lili's hands like water. By the time I came to live in Abergavenny Lili was long gone from the town, seduced by an Italian Lothario and running his ice-cream business somewhere in the Valleys. By then Mum couldn't remember exactly where, nor could she think of his surname, though a card came for her every Christmas with a smudged postmark, kisses from Lili and Guiseppe and an awful lot of glitter.

'Your cousin Lili was a one,' was all my mother would say, with a faraway look in her eyes, and I had to stop myself from saying something mean. I would have liked to have had my hair done in a beehive, but Mum thought hair lacquer was 'bad for the air.' It wasn't that my mother was an environmentalist before her time, she just hated the thought of me having something that she couldn't have.

I have sometimes wondered whether Lili really did go to see the Beatles or whether she made the whole thing up.

The Friday women

One thing I know to be true is that it was friends of Lili's who set up the women's walking group which, in the fullness of time when I came to live in Abergavenny, would be my lifeline. By the late 1970s those women, unlike my flighty cousin, had settled down with the husband and 2.5 children of the time. When the children started school and they had some time for themselves again, a few of them started walking together every Friday. The few grew into more and then many, a network of women in Abergavenny and around.

They met in one another's houses for coffee before setting off up the Deri, or the Rholben or a further hill. They were spoilt for choice; one of them told me when I eventually joined them that you could do a different walk on the Sugar Loaf and its foothills every week of the year. Up there amongst the bracken and the wimberry bushes they would sit and eat their sandwiches before heading back in time to pick up the children from school. This was before the red kites came back to our skies, but there were small birds a-plenty, wild horses too. They formed strong bonds, these women, but ones which were elastic enough to embrace newcomers to the town.

One of the newcomers was called Inga. She had come from Norway. She went to the hair salon where Lili worked.

'You should meet my friends,' Lili said when Inga asked about things going on in the town and said she enjoyed walking.

I heard about Inga from Lili the next Christmas. Apparently she had a ring in her nose.

'Like the piggywig in The Owl and the Pussycat!' I said.

Lili said it wasn't in the end of her nose, but anyway. She had had her suspicions about Inga and it turned out that she was right. When Inga joined the women's walking group everyone loved her. She brought Norwegian cakes and difference. None of the Abergavenny women could afford foreign holidays at that time and Inga brought the foreign to them. Not with her colourful clothes and braided hair, they were all a bit hippy-ish, but she had something dangerous about her. And they flirted with it. As she flirted with their husbands, when Christmas came, the season of parties when alcohol loosened everything. There were so many stories, no doubt exaggerated in the telling and re-telling before they reached me from Lili.

'So, you won't be so popular now?' I asked Lili. 'You pointed her in their direction.'

Lili paused in combing out Mum's hair—she always did it at Christmas, bless her—only long enough to shrug her shoulders.

'Not my fault,' she said.

I was living in London by that time, but I was restless. I yearned for something else but I didn't know where to go. Hearing Lili's stories about these women made me wonder. What if I was to move to Abergavenny? But I wasn't yet 30. This was a small town and it's a big world. It was too soon for me, I knew. I didn't say anything to my cousin. And a lot would change for both of us before I made that move.

One out, another in

Five years later Lili met Guiseppe, her ice-cream dream. They had the proverbial whirlwind romance, of which Mum disapproved, but she and I went over to the wedding. The reception was to be held in a big hotel in the centre of Abergavenny and family guests were put up there. Dead posh venue, according to what Bronwen had told Mum. Apparently the Beatles had stayed there after that gig in 1963. I don't know what it was like then but I thought it was pretty scruffy in 1985. Mum did too—ran her finger along the windowsill in her room and held it up in triumphant horror at the dust. There were hairs in the plug hole of the bath and a dusty grey sock under my bed.

But the wedding was lovely. They had the service in the Baptist church and then we all went back to the posh hotel for the reception. We walked there through town behind the bride and groom—Lili looked peachy in her big white frock and Guiseppe was very dashing, they made a lovely couple. People on the street cheered as if they were local royalty and threw confetti, and I felt so happy for Lili. There was a ballroom in the hotel with a little balcony. After we'd all had a few drinks Guiseppe went up there and serenaded Lili. So sweet. Except halfway through his song he gave a strangled cry, his head disappeared from view and a cloud of confetti dropped over the diners. Plaster confetti. A few more bottles of bubbly appeared, on the house, and the celebrations continued as if nothing had happened. But my mum was annoyed. As Lili had obviously been a bit busy before the wedding, Mum had had to pay someone else to do her hair and now it was ruined by the plaster dust.

'Give over, Mum,' I said. 'It'll comb out. And anyway, no-one's looking at you.'

Mum got all huffy with me, but next morning she'd forgotten all about it and as we strolled through the town it became evident that she had something else on her mind.

'I'm going to move here,' she announced to me. 'Keep Bronwen company, now Lili's spoken for.'

'But what about Ron?' I was taken aback. 'You used to say–'

'Never mind what I used to say,' she said. 'And, anyway, I'm not moving in with Bron and Ron. I'll get my own place. A flat.'

I didn't know what to say. It was true that I'd vaguely thought about moving to Abergavenny myself a few years before, but I definitely didn't want to do so then. It wasn't just the hotel that was scruffy; everything and everyone on the street that morning had looked drab and dull compared with the lights and sparkle of London. On the other hand the thought of travelling back and forth to South Wales to visit Mum didn't appeal either.

'I'm not asking you to come,' Mum said, as if reading my mind. 'You go on your fancy travels. Don't worry about me.'

She had this way of flicking her eyes. I knew she didn't mean what she said. But I took her at her word and, after she'd moved, I didn't visit. I'd get pathetic phone calls from her asking if I remembered I had a mum, but I steeled myself against them. I led my life and she led hers. I travelled, I had fun, and Abergavenny, that little town at the foot of a mountain that some said was full of water, played no part in my life. I didn't know much about what Mum did, and at that time no news was good news as far as I was concerned.

Bronwen

It's a right turn-up, my big sister deciding she's going to come and live in little old Abergavenny, as she used to describe it, with one of her nose-in-the-air sniffs. She would never ever come here for Christmas, though you wouldn't have thought that would be too much to ask given that Ron always has to work over other people's holidays. They want their milk, and there aren't many proper milkmen left. Gwladys says you can buy milk in a shop and that may be so, but what about the poor old dears who can't get out I say to her, she'll be like that one day and then she'll see. Though I suppose, being Gwlad, she'll still expect someone to fetch and carry for her. But she's still my sister and blood matters so Lili and I would trail across the country every Christmas, which was never easy on the trains. But anyway.

Lili liked seeing her cousin and they'd go to Megan's room and talk for hours, goodness knows what stories Lili told her she always did, you might say, fancy things up. Like when the Beatles came to Abergavenny and she was desperate to go but Ron said he wasn't having any daughter of his throwing her knickers at men with long hair—he used another word about them too which I am not going to repeat—and I asked him how he could even suggest such a thing our Lili was not that kind of girl but he put his foot down. Lili was that upset and afterwards she read about it in the local paper and she'd recite the details as if she'd really been there.

I did feel sorry for Gwlad after her husband went off with that woman he met in a pub, I mean what was he doing going out to pubs at night leaving his wife and a young kid at home, but that was him so good riddance, I said, but Gwlad was funny, she would still stick up for him and say it must have been hard for a man, working all day and coming home to a demanding child. I told her, Gwlad, you put up with the child all day long, wipe its bottom and everything, that man never did that did he, but she said that was her duty. It made me mad, her being like that. I don't know what Megan thinks about it all, she doesn't seem to have a young man, maybe she's turned against them what a shame if so because there are some decent men out there. My Ron is good as they come, solid Valleys boy, Tredegar born and bred where Nye Bevan came from, that great man who created our National Health Service what would we do without it. And our Lili has landed on her feet with Guiseppe, he's a gentleman. None of us will ever go without ice-cream or cwtches now that he's part of the family, I'm so happy to have such a wonderful son-in-law.

Cherry blossom and lilacs

Gwladys Pritchard set out as usual to go to her Wednesday coffee club. She put on her good winter coat, hat and gloves. There had been snow that winter, so pretty on the hills from her windows but she knew she had to wrap up. They were always saying so at the club, and of course she was nearly 80. It was marked on the calendar somewhere, though she couldn't really believe she was that old.

As she opened the door of her flat Gwladys was surprised to see a cherry tree in the garden in blossom. It was definitely too early for flowers to be out. She felt snug and warm in her good coat. The streets were completely clear of snow. That surprised her too. When she saw that there were trees in blossom in all the gardens along Belgrave Road she was even more surprised.

At the club they had the windows open.

'Take your coat off Gwladys,' said one of the helpers. She was called Maureen, or possibly Mavis. Whichever it was, Gwladys found her very bossy.

'Come on lovely,' the Maureen/Mavis woman said. 'You'll boil in that heavy coat!'

Gwladys did not like being called 'lovely', and she did not want to take her coat off. She wanted to ask what on earth they were doing flinging the windows open in January, they'd all catch their deaths, but she was, in truth, a little scared of the bossy woman.

'I'll keep my coat on, thank you,' she said, pulling it round her and biting her lip.

'And it's two sugars,' she said as Maureen/Mavis plonked a cup in front of her, spilling tea into the saucer. The helper sighed, turned to her friend and said something that Gwladys couldn't hear. Then they both sniggered.

Gwladys felt something rising in her chest. She wanted to cry. Someone on her left was spooning sugar into her tea.

'Don't you fret, Mrs P.' It was a young man. She didn't much like being called Mrs P but it was better than 'lovely'.

'They don't mean no harm,' he said. 'But you will be awfully hot if you keep your coat on.'

Someone else was pulling out the keyboard which they used for Christmas carols.

'Are we singing Christmas carols?' Gwladys said to the young man. He looked like the son she wished she'd had. She only had a daughter, one who didn't seem to care about her any more. That made her want to cry too, thinking about Megan.

The young man was laughing, but in a kindly way.

'Are you my long-lost son?' she said to him.

He patted her knee. 'Maybe so,' he said, with a twinkle in his eye. 'I'm sure you're a lovely mum. But no, no carols Mrs P. We've visitors.'

Gwladys looked across the room and there was a girl, a good bit younger than her Megan, talking to a man who was sitting down at the keyboard now.

'They're going to serenade us,' the young man said.

A ssshhh went round the room and someone shut the kitchen door. Gwladys felt a breeze through the window and unbuttoned her coat as the girl began to sing. A song about spring, happy and sad at the same time. As she listened Gwladys felt a weight begin to lift off her chest.

There was a song to join in with, one from Ivor Novello, the famous Welsh composer, the girl was saying, they probably all knew the words, but there were song sheets if they needed them. 'We'll Gather Lilacs' - oh yes, they did all know the words. It was from that time before Gwladys was married, oh, what memories. Dances every Friday, so many young men, she could have had her pick of half a dozen. Gwladys was crying now, but they were happy tears. The girl, the singer, was there amongst them, asking if they'd enjoyed it.

'It was–' Gwladys paused. Could she say this, choked as she was? 'It was marvellous,' she said. 'You took me back to the best time of my life.'

Now there was a tear in the girl's eye. She took Gwladys' hands in her own, small and unlined ones, and crouched down beside her.

'Thank you so much,' she said. 'I'm so glad.'

When Gwladys got home she looked at her calendar and found it was April, not January, and that in three days' time it would be her birthday. She wondered whether Megan would remember.

Bronwen

Gwlad's been here nearly a year now and she seems to have settled in nicely. Goes to the Priory Church, St Mary's. Good luck to you, I said and she said Whad'you mean? and I wasn't going to say it, but whatever, I can't be doing with all that business of the minister changing vestments three times in a service and swinging incense, gets right up my nose. I go to the Baptists, genuine people they are, can't do enough for you, we had such a lovely service for Lili's wedding. Simple, that's what I like. Nice straightforward hymns and more Welsh I always think. Anglicans are English, but then Gwlad is more English than Welsh really, lived over there all that time and if the way that Anglicans do things suits her that's fine by me. She's met people there, I don't know whether they're proper friends, but no matter, she has coffee with them after church and one of them has told her about a coffee club somewhere else in the week. Stops her ringing me fussing about how lonely I must be now Lili's gone. Which I am not. Lili rings me every Sunday, she's a good girl, always has been. I'm just hoping that, well, some day soon there will be a little one on the way, after all they've been married eighteen months, long enough for you know, and her not in the first flush, no time to waste. Me and Ron would love to be grandparents.

Gwlad says that her Megan has gone travelling but when I ask her where she doesn't seem to know, which makes me feel just a little bit annoyed with that girl. Though, like I say, blood matters, so I'll forgive her. The young need to follow their dreams, though come to think of it Megan's well into her thirties same as our Lili, time she thought about settling down somewhere, though if she can't find a nice young man. I really don't know why she wouldn't, she's a plain girl but some men like that, must do by the looks of the wedding photos in the local paper.

I walk my dog—Daisy, she's a wire-haired fox terrier, lovely little thing, like a fluffy teddy bear—twice a day, gets me out and in the fresh air. We go up through the fields at the bottom of the Deri and Daisy can run free when there aren't any sheep. She loves a ball.

I've tried to get Gwlad to come out with us but she says Daisy might trip her up which is just plain stupid. I don't like to think of my big sister losing her confidence, but we're none of us getting any younger. Makes me shiver to think about what might happen in the future so I don't. Turn my mind to what to cook Ron for his tea. Maybe sausages today, he loves those. From the butchers, with mash and peas. Tasty iawn, as the Welsh say.

We haven't seen Megan for so long now. Gwlad says she has no clue where she is, never writes, never phones. I find it shocking that a girl can neglect her mother like that. For two pins I'd ring her up and say so except Ron says not to, there might be an explanation.

And it looks like there is. It seems I might have been a bit hard on Megan. When I went in to see her mum today I found a whole pile of postcards, from Rome and Ibiza and all sorts of places I'd never even heard of, gosh. Turns out they're all from Meg.

'Goodness, Gwlad, your girl must have been all round the world!' I say to her.

But when I put the postcards in front of her she looks at them as if she's never seen them before. And she is getting muddled, told me last week that she hadn't any eggs, so I got some from the lady that supplies Ron for his round and blow me, Gwlad's got not just six but two dozen in her fridge when I come to look. Not that my memory's what it was, I'm always looking around for my door key or my specs, but forget I had eggs in the fridge—never! And I'm wondering whether with Gwlad it isn't just about forgetting the odd thing, I've got this really awful feeling and I can't seem to shake it off.

A phone call

'Hello, Megan.'

The voice on the line was unfamiliar.

'Who's this?' I said, thinking at first that it was a cold caller. It was years since I'd spoken to my aunt.

'It's about your mum,' she said.

'What's happened to her?' I was, suddenly and unexpectedly, terrified that my mum, who I barely thought about but knew was there and assumed was always going to be there, was going to die. Perhaps had already died. My heart lurched.

'Your mum,' she said, 'has got a birthday coming up and she's going to be 80. I'm organising a party. Surprise, like. I know you have your own life but I want you to come. This once. Because–' The line went silent.

'Because what, Aunty Bronwen?' Now I was panicking.

'The thing is,' she said, and then there was another long pause and a sigh before she eventually continued.

'I'm worried about her, Megan.' And she told me why.

Learning the truth

I arrived in Abergavenny by train on a sunny Thursday morning. The town looked so different from that day, nearly fifteen years before, when I'd strolled through the dowdy streets with Mum after Lili's wedding. Now, as I walked towards the centre from the station, the hills standing sentinel were crisp cut-outs against the blue sky, I could understand the legends—that the Blorenge to the south, with its distinctive blancmange shape, was full of water, and that the Sugar Loaf peak ahead of her was the cone of an ancient volcano.

When I reached the hotel where we'd had Lili's wedding reception I could hardly believe it was the same place. It was newly painted, brass plates on the doors polished and shining. Inside, I could see, there was a huge vase of white lilies on the reception desk. Someone came out as I stood there and held the door open for me, but I shook my head. This time the hotel was not my destination. I carried on, down Frogmore Street, where there were at least two new gift shops and lots of cafes. At the War Memorial—still on the lean, they hadn't repaired that, I noticed—I turned right, then left up Pen-y-Pound and found myself passing the town football field where John Lennon had reportedly arrived by helicopter in 1963.

I stopped to check the map and found that this was not the way to the Mardy, I'd taken the wrong turning. Had to retrace my steps, go left and left again and I was on the right road then, heading up past the Leisure Centre and the Grammar School, King Henry VIII. I remembered Lili talking about it. What had become of Lili, I wondered. And now I had reached the area called The Mardy. I'd never been there before, had thought from its name it was a village, but no, it was rows and rows of semi-detached houses. Just like those London suburbs that you went through on trains, glad you didn't live there as you looked at their tiny back gardens, cheek by jowl. Little boxes, like in the song Pete Seeger used to sing. That would have been about the same time that the Beatles came to Abergavenny, funny the connections you make in your mind.

I stopped, out of breath from the incline. I didn't get much exercise in London. Above the houses of the Mardy I could see a path curving through the dried bracken onto the Deri, and the beginnings of this year's new growth, touches of bright green. There was a movement up there and, for a moment, the distinct profile of a deer. The thought went through my head that it would be good to be able to walk on that hill. All the places I'd lived had been so flat. There was some part of me that craved another landscape. Maybe, I thought, this town, nestled in these hills?

But that was a question for another day. I was at Bronwen's door. There were six gnomes on my aunt's doorstep and my cousin Lili flicking back the lace curtain and grinning at me, and then a little face next to her, the spit of her mum. Somewhere in the house a dog was barking, and Uncle Ron was opening the door and Guiseppe was behind him and gathering me up in a big Welsh cwtch.

It was lovely to see them all, it had been so long. The rest of that day passed in 'Do you remember when this?' and 'What about the time when,' and then, after we'd eaten local faggots—still the same butchers, said Bronwen, you will have passed them in town on your way up Megan—and my aunt's famous wimberry pie—we saved the berries from last year, she said—we eased ourselves back on the big leather sofas that Lili had bought for her mum and, finally, talked about *my* mum.

'Some days she seems totally fine,' Bronwen said. 'And you wouldn't think that there was anything up with her at all. But you'll notice the difference Megan, you really will.'

The pull of the hills

The surprise party was planned for the Saturday. Lili said she was going to meet up with her old friends in the walking group for coffee on the Friday morning, her mum was looking after the kids, why didn't I come along? I might even fancy going for a walk with them, not that you'll catch me doing that, said Lili. I could see what her mother meant when she said that her daughter had become a 'comfortable' size since she'd had children. Walking was something which she did as far as the car, no further.

The Friday was another beautiful Spring day. Lili drove us down the old Hereford Road into town, and round to a house in Western Road.

'Your mum lives near here,' said Lili, giving me a quick, sharp look. I shrank back in my seat. Lili didn't say so, and neither did Bronwen, but I could tell they took a dim view of my never visiting Mum.

We could hear the hubbub in the house from the street. In the hallway was a scatter of anoraks, walking boots and sticks.

'Hi Fiona,' Lili called to a woman who'd arrived just before us. 'This is my cousin Megan, down from London. Tell her what's what, will you?'

Lili disappeared into another room; I could hear her high giggles as she greeted old chums. Someone poured me a coffee. Fiona introduced me to people whose names I promptly forgot. The room was crowded, the laughter loud. It was all I could do to keep my head above the waves of the conversations that flowed back and forth and swirled around the kitchen. Far from the hippies I'd heard of years before, these women seemed more like Amazons. I really wasn't sure I would be able to keep up with them on the hills, said as much when someone asked if I was joining them on the walk, but they were so encouraging, all these Sues and Amandas and Marys and more, that before I knew it I'd been lent boots and a stick and had set out with them towards one of those Sugar Loaf foothills.

It was the most glorious day for a walk, and there was something magical about these hills. It wasn't just that people said that—I could feel it. And my muscles responded to the unaccustomed challenge. Later they would ache, no doubt, but this felt, well, right.

We stopped for lunch in a little sheltered hollow. After we'd eaten, someone suggested we sit in silence for a few minutes and I lay back on the dry bracken, closed my eyes, listened to the wind and the birdsong and felt that little bit closer to whatever heaven might be.

When we got back into Abergavenny I had, without meaning to or even consciously doing so, made a decision. I was going to sell my flat in London and move to this town that—I learned this on the walk—had seven hills. I didn't say that to any of the other women on that day, but several of them told me later they were not surprised, that Abergavenny was a kind of magnet, and I was just one of the many people attracted to it.

'So, when are you going round to see your poor old mum?' my aunt said when I got back from the walk. 'Or are you planning to just turn up at the party and pretend you haven't neglected her all this time?' Her voice was sharp.

I went round to Mum's the next morning. We sat awkwardly for a while with our cups of tea, nibbling politely on the Welsh cakes which I'd taken as a peace offering. She asked me about London and my travels and I told her some of it, not all, after all who does that with their mother, however well they get on?

I said what a beautiful view she had from her window over the Sugar Loaf and its foothills, and she got quite animated then and told me their names, all of them bang on and said yes, she was lucky. I knew in the silence that followed that she wanted to say something like how much luckier she'd be if her daughter visited more often. I could have told her then of my decision, but it was too soon for either of us. Not that I could see anything wrong with Mum's memory, which was a big relief. It seemed to me then that my aunt had been exaggerating.

She certainly put on a great spread for the birthday party. The pièce de resistance was an ice-cream cake from Guiseppe, with sparklers. Mum clapped her hands like a five-year-old and smiles rippled round the room. People had come from her coffee club and they all got tiddly on ginger wine. Lili and I were drinking Prosecco. In 1999 hardly anyone in Wales or England had even heard of it, but Guiseppe had got hold of decent Italian stuff and it made our evening go by in a happy haze.

On the Sunday I called round to see Mum again before heading back to London. She said it had been a lovely party.

'Do you really have to go?'

'Yes, Mum, I've got to be at work tomorrow. But I'll be back soon.'

I could see she didn't believe me, but I was going to prove her wrong.

A different world

I was true to my word. In the optimistic early days of the new Millennium I put my flat in London on the market and rented a cottage near the river in Llanwenarth, a little village just outside Abergavenny. From my kitchen window I looked out onto the trees on the lower slopes of the Blorenge. I'd been in the cottage two weeks when a black cat appeared at the back door. No-one came to claim him. I called him Percy and he sat on my knee in front of the wood-burning stove every evening. I'd always wanted a cat, but Mum wouldn't hear of it when I was a child, she hated the smell, and in a London flat it's hopeless.

The months passed quickly. Some people say that it always rains in Wales but the first summer I was in Abergavenny the weather was balmy. I took my supper out to the rickety wooden table under the apple tree in my garden every evening. As I ate Percy would sit by my side quietly. He was not a greedy cat. He didn't ask for titbits, just my company. And I was content with his.

'Don't expect this to happen again!' people said. For it was, they said, unheard-of for the weather to be this good, for this long.

Percy would come with me when I walked down to the river after supper as the light faded on the Blorenge. Sometimes there was the flash of a kingfisher, or the slow lift-off of the night heron that waded down there. London seemed to exist in a different world. And it was true that Abergavenny was the world for me now. I did not need anywhere beyond this town and its surrounding hills where I could walk whenever I wanted, with others or alone.

Most of the time you see no-one when you're out walking on these hills, you're alone with the sheep and the birds and, in some places, the wild horses, but the first time I went up the Sugar Loaf on my own I saw a man on the path behind me, and wondered whether, after all, I was being foolhardy. All the way up I could see him, following. I could have changed my mind, taken a different route, but what if he had followed? I could have tried to hide in the bracken, but my mind was teeming with what ifs now. I carried on, puffing up the final steep stretch to the grassy summit. I sat down with my back to the trig point, pulled my water pot from my bag and gazed out over the sculpted lines of Pen-y-Fan to the West, awaiting my fate.

'Hello,' said the man. 'Beautiful up here, isn't it? Mind if I–?' he said, gesturing to the space next to me.

What could I do? He looked perfectly normal, like any other walker.

'Do you live here?' he said.

I nodded.

'God, you're so lucky,' he said, holding something out to me.

'Lucky you're not out to murder me?' I said. It was a stupid thing to say, especially when someone's just offered you chocolate. Fortunately he laughed. Pity he was just visiting. One of the few drawbacks of a small town like Abergavenny is that you don't come across too many single men, up mountains or anywhere else.

New connections

The internet had made it possible to work from home by this time, though once a week I took the train up to London for the day, went into the office and had lunch with my old friends. I found that I was always glad to get back on the train in the evening, to be leaving the grime of the city and returning to Abergavenny. On Tuesdays I walked along the river to do my shopping at the Market and visited Mum while I was in town. We got on fine if we only saw one another once a week. I could see now that her memory wasn't what it had been, but I made sure she had lists of everything she had to do and she seemed to be coping just fine. I knew a young man from her coffee club kept an eye on her, and he'd have let me know if he had any concerns, surely.

I organised my work so that most Fridays I could walk with the women. Over the next two years I got to know the hills around the town really well. Every week one woman or another on the walk would remark on how lucky we were to live where we did, and I did feel it was so. We walked on the Blorenge, up the steep incline with its clear evidence of the old iron workings, and along a high tramroad which led to a place called The Punchbowl. As we sat on the edge of that still water having lunch and dragonflies danced before us, I knew it to be a special place. I could well imagine the surface of the lake being broken by an arm rising up holding a sword. But the only creatures making ripples that day were ducks.

We walked on the Skirrid, the Holy Mountain where on Good Friday every year people used to drag up a heavy cross to the stones of the old chapel on the summit. We walked on myriad paths up the Sugar Loaf. We watched salmon leaping at Llangenny in the late autumn and gazed on view upon view over these border hills. In summer there were those who would strip off and swim in the river waters. I did not do that, though on the rare occasions in winter when it was possible I would lie down and make a snow angel with my arms and legs.

These were charmed days, the hills providing a balm to soothe whatever ills or worries beset any of us. Most of us had ageing parents. Some had wayward teenagers or husbands. I asked about Inga, the woman I had heard about from Lili, the one who had flirted with some of the husbands. Or more, Lili had implied. Oh, they said, with a small laugh or in some cases a grimace, she had moved on, it had been years now since they'd seen her.

And then she came back. I was the one who opened the door to her.

'Ah,' I said, 'Inga. I've heard about you.'

As the words fell from my mouth I knew it was a foolish thing to say, but then I was a newcomer, it was fair enough that I would have heard of lots of people but not met them yet. But her smile had a hardness to it. I did not pursue the conversation beyond the usual pleasantries. Why she had come was not clear. It was, she said, a holiday, but she upset things, turning up like that. And it was no doubt fanciful of me to associate the two, but the weather turned with her arrival, the day became squally as did relations amongst the women. After that walk a feeling of unease spread through the group. There were factions. But we got through it, pulled back together because we could still talk to one another. Which was a mercy, because from time to time I definitely needed people I could talk to about Mum.

A one-way journey

It was in the November of the year after Megan moved to the cottage that Gwladys had her first fall.

'What's that bruise on your leg, Mum?' Megan said, pausing halfway across the room.

'Nothing,' said Gwladys. 'Don't fuss and stop looking so worried. I told you, it's nothing.'

'You fussed when I was little.'

'But *I'm* not little, so don't do it.'

Gwladys didn't know how she'd fallen or remember it actually happening; she'd just found herself on the floor of her kitchen. Her left hip was sore and she thought she'd probably hit it on the edge of the table. She was not going to tell her daughter this, because she was scared. Not scared of the bruises; she'd ridden horses when she was a girl in North Wales and had learned how to fall. But scared that Megan would say that she'd have to have people in. Gwladys had a horror of having to have people look after her. It was okay the young man from the coffee club coming by, she couldn't think of his name. Except he fussed a bit too much. Like Megan, who'd left her alone for years and now was breathing down her neck all the time. Gwladys couldn't be doing with fuss.

'I can look after myself, Megan,' said Gwladys.

'It's all very well you saying that, Mum. But I'm going to get the doctor in to check you over,' said Megan.

'I think we'd better get the home care people in for a little chat,' said the doctor.

'We can send someone in twice a week,' said the home care supervisor. 'Just to give you a bit of help. Don't you think so, lovely?'

Gwladys shrugged her shoulders and turned her head to the window. Up on the hill there were horses. She leaned forward to see them better and watched them as they galloped free.

'You didn't have to be so rude to the lady,' Megan said after the home care person had gone. 'You should be grateful.'

Bronwen

I can't understand why Megan didn't tell me about her mum falling over. I could go round more often, look after her a bit, I don't like the thought of those care people, you don't know who they are, we never would have allowed that with our mam, God rest her soul she died before either Megan or Lili was born but in those days it was family did the caring, same with Ron's family in the Valleys. Like I always say blood matters.

But the younger generation isn't like that, I'm just glad that me and Ron are hale and hearty because I can't see Lili and Guiseppe wanting to come back to Abergavenny. Okay, give her credit, Megan has come to live here, that really did surprise me, but it's not because of her mum and she's not going to do what I did and our mam before me, they see things differently now, be near but separate Megan says, some such talk. To me we're all connected and that's the right thing, and I'd have Gwlad move in with us except it's a small house and anyway she wouldn't want it, what she wants is her independence and I do see that.

But carers, people she doesn't know, thank goodness it's just shopping and a bit of cleaning as far as I understand, not personal stuff, Gwladys wouldn't be happy with strangers doing that any more than I would, though of course it may come to that, God help us, but sadly prayers to the Lord, whether you're with the Baptists or the Anglicans, are not going to make the smallest scrap of difference to the way my poor sister is going.

Cows and sheep

I was cautious about joining in with anything in the town for the first year or two, apart from the women's walking group. It's a small town. If you join something and then it doesn't suit you it's difficult to pull away. It was different in London, where you could stay anonymous. I knew there was lots going on in Abergavenny, but I was happy, in those early days, to be an observer.

A cattle market was still held in the centre of town on Tuesdays, as it had been for over 150 years. Some people complained about the smell of the animals. I didn't mind that, though I felt sorry for the sheep penned up awaiting their fate. But the market, like my mother, was in decline. What had been the whole raison d'être for the town of Abergavenny would close, it was only a matter of time. There was a campaign to save it, I saw people handing out leaflets, but I avoided them. From what I read in the local paper, it was a battle which had been lost before I ever arrived in the town.

I tended to avoid the coffee stall in the corner of the Market Hall on Farmers' Market days, because the leaflet people were part of that. I didn't want to get sucked in. But one day I went over and chatted and no-one tried to get me to sign anything. They did say they were awfully short of helpers, they were all volunteers. I found myself saying well, once a month wasn't a lot, would a couple of hours be any use? I could manage that, just so long as I didn't have to go to any meetings, I'd had enough of all that.

'That's brilliant, thank you so much. By the way, have you seen our sheep?' they said.

Oh yes, I said, I'd been to the cattle market.

'No, no,' they said, pointing up, '*these* sheep!'

I looked up. There was a flock of them hanging above me. Rag-rugged sheep and crocheted lambs. Made, they said, for the Food Festival.

The town was one of the first to have such a festival, apparently. It was brilliant, they said, and there was this whole group of volunteers who made the decorations. Each year they were different, and they stayed up in the Market Hall all year. The latest Food Festival had just happened, what a shame I'd missed it, they said. There was a community feast too when the new decorations were lit up, the only time in the year that happened. Next year, they said, look out for the details in the paper.

I took myself back to the cottage and my cat Percy before I found myself volunteering for more than I really wanted to. But it was good to know about these things that were going on in the town, and that in the fullness of time I could, if I felt like it, get more involved in them.

Not really a love affair

By the summer of 2004 I decided that I could afford to work part-time. I was well settled in Abergavenny now, confident in giving directions to tourists and feeling the sort of satisfaction that comes from being a resident rather than a visitor, the sort of feet-under-the-table comfort of it. Mum had accepted home care, and that seemed to be keeping her on an even keel. As far as I knew.

I was happy in the cottage near the river, happy for it to be just me and Percy, and happy helping on the coffee stall at the Farmers' Market for a few hours once a month. Happy enough. But I wanted something more, something to stretch me. I was only too aware that, although you didn't hear people speaking it in the streets of Abergavenny, Wales had its own language. Of which, at that point I knew no more than the word for 'thank you' —'diolch'. 'Please' in Welsh was something longer than I couldn't get my tongue or my head around. I felt faintly ashamed of this.

One of the women in the walking group ran her own little Welsh class every summer, just for a week, a taster you might say, so I went along. Elin, the woman was called. She had a cat called Tomos, and he would sit on my knee and purr loudly in my ear. I enjoyed that more than the Welsh, but Elin encouraged me, said I could be really good, why not go to the intensive summer school in the Hill College in Abergavenny, then I'd be well ahead when classes started in September.

Flattery has often been my undoing. I signed up for the summer school. It was very jolly and utterly terrifying.

'Sut wyt ti?' said a voice behind me as I walked back down the hill into town. I knew it meant "How are you?"

'Er, er, iawn, diolch,' I said, 'I'm fine,' looking round to to see my class tutor, Rhodri.

'Bendigedig,' he said, grinning. 'Excellent, you are already!'

I didn't feel excellent. I was exhausted and floundering in all the different ways of saying 'yes' and 'no' in Welsh.

'It's really hard,' I said.

'I know. Look,' he hesitated. 'Do you fancy going for a drink? Unless–'

My turn to hesitate.

'I don't know anyone in Abergavenny,' he said, pulling a 'poor-me' sort of face. 'I'm all on my own in a B&B. Not huge fun.'

I wasn't sure this was a good idea, but next thing I was walking into a pub in town with him and saying that a glass of white would be great, yes please, 'gwin gwyn'. Except I pronounced it the wrong way round and I could feel myself blushing. I hoped to goodness this didn't make him think I fancied him. And then to make matters even worse I found myself telling him about Mum.

'You really don't want to hear all this,' I said after a bit.

'No, no, I do,' he said. 'I know what it's like. My mother went the same way. For ages she was just fine, managing with someone going in to her a couple of times a week, and then, all of a sudden, she got so much worse. She was ringing me up asking why she never saw me when I'd been in the day before.'

I drained my glass and didn't argue when Rhodri jumped up to get me another. Looking around, I noticed two of the women from the walking group in a corner. Oh well, so there would be gossip. That's the way of a small town. Let them say what they wanted, I thought.

Rhodri and I met a time or two after that but it didn't come to much. It certainly didn't merit the term relationship, and as he wasn't married it couldn't be called an affair. I think that disappointed the gossip-mongers, but I didn't mind. And my love affair with Welsh was equally short-lived, which also disappointed some of the walking group women, I think.

31

Doubts

The following winter Mum had several falls, and getting extra care sorted out was a major headache, especially as I seemed to pick up every virus going and had less than no energy for anything. I missed the women's walks week after week. Some of the women sought me out though, and we'd meet up for coffee. They told me about a drumming group but that really wasn't my thing. Nor was knitting. I joined a reading group though, and gradually acquaintances turned into real friends.

That June I went to France for a fortnight to visit old friends. When I came back I found Mum in good spirits. We managed several days out—to Brecon, Hay, and a garden full of heady scents somewhere in a maze of country lanes. It felt, for that brief period, as if we had turned back time. As Mum and I sat together in a courtyard cafe on a July morning of pale sunlight, she said, out of the blue:

'It's a Lady of the Bedchamber to the Queen.'

'What? Who?' I looked around but we were the only people there. So this was the next stage of her illness, hallucinations. I shivered, though the day was warm.

'She's died,' said Mum. 'It was on the news.'

'Uh-huh,' I said.

'Yes,' she insisted. 'The Marchioness of Abergavenny.'

I laughed at the sheer ludicrousness of Mum coming up with this snippet, and relief that she wasn't going barmy, well, no more barmy than she was already. Except.

'What's so funny?' she said. 'You shouldn't laugh about people dying. I suppose you'll laugh when *I* die.'

We had an argument and the spell of summer was broken. It turned out to be the last fine day, followed by weeks of rain. As I watched the water flooding over the meadow and into my little garden, I remembered what people had said that first summer of endless sunshine, about not expecting it to happen again.

I've never liked walking in the rain. I missed more walks and didn't even join the women for coffee. My weekly visits to Mum were as short as I could make them, the ease of our summer days together gone. I switched on the answerphone and didn't return calls. I began to feel that coming to this corner of Wales had been a mistake. I missed all the things that went on in London, choosing to forget that most of the time I hadn't been to any of those things. But then something changed, the way things do, unexpectedly, and for the better.

Working in the chicken factory

I got an e-mail. It contained an open invitation to attend workshops to make decorations for the forthcoming Abergavenny Food Festival. The theme this year, they said, would be Giant Chickens, Cockerels and Chicks. It was, the message continued, a very special year, the 10th anniversary of the Festival there would be fireworks and much razzmatazz. They wanted as many people as possible who had sewing or making skills to take part. I wasn't too sure about my sewing skills or whether I was capable of making anything, but it felt like a rope thrown to a drowning person, this invitation. Something told me that if I didn't grab hold of it I would quite simply sink beneath the rising waters which would one day burst from the foot of the Blorenge.

So, I went along on the first morning, to an old school in Abergavenny which had been turned into an Arts Centre. I didn't know the place existed, had never been down that road even. And I didn't recognise any of the people gathered in the room.

'Would you like coffee?' The woman looked frighteningly arty, but I liked her immediately. Perhaps because she, the one in charge of all this making-to-come, was also the one making everyone coffee and cutting up a cake she'd made that morning.

'I'm not sure if I'm going to be much help.' I said.

'Don't worry.' She laughed, but not in a dismissive way. 'We'll just be rolling up paper balls to start with. I'm Theresa by the way.'

And that was what we did that first day, me and the others. Rolled up paper balls to stick over the cardboard forma that Theresa cut out, to start making the shapes of the chickens. By five o'clock there were already several huge creatures taking shape and we all went home in a flurry of 'See you tomorrow!'.

Over the next three weeks I became immersed in the making, relegating my paid work to evenings. Apart from Tuesdays, when I called in to see Mum and did my shopping at the market, I was in the chicken factory every day. But this was a very different kind of chicken factory from the one which I'd been told was on the western side of the Skirrid. This was a place of creativity and fun. And when those birds got their feathers it was difficult to believe that they were made from strips of silks and gauze, that their coxcombs and the wattles hanging from their chins were red serge, their sharp beaks cardboard and—the touch which finally brought them alive—their shining black eyes painted and varnished ping-pong balls.

At about one o'clock each day space was cleared on the tables and we sat down to share food. People made late summer crops of tomatoes, courgettes and apples from their gardens into salads and tarts, both savoury and sweet; brought meats, cheeses, bread. Every day there would be some new deliciousness at those lunches. And from time to time throughout the day, the call would go up:

'Who's for tea?'

'Lapsang, please,' would come the muffled reply from someone lying on the floor stitching the underside of a bird, or 'Earl Grey for me' shouted from the far end of the room.

There was always cake and always laughter, even when one of us found we had sewn an entire wing of feathers the wrong way round, or our backs ached from sewing all afternoon at a strange angle. How Theresa managed to stay so calm through those weeks amazed me. She never knew how many people would turn up and whether they could cut or sew or paint with any proficiency at all. There was so much to do in really so little time. And then near the end a phalanx of others would turn up, keen to be part of the process, and the room would get so full that I'd resort to sewing in a corridor.

Somehow everything was finished in time for the birds to be bundled into vans by lads from the Food Festival, who took them to the Market Hall for the hanging. This involved immensely strong nylon cord, a man up a cherry picker and Theresa directing operations from below. It went on late into the night. When everyone arrived for the Fanfare Feast the following evening the big birds were flying, the baby chicks running in the air and all of us in the team—for we had become one—were so happy and proud. There was a little bit of me up there; I felt that I was, after all, beginning to feel at home in this town.

Revenge is sweet

It was the Saturday morning of the Food Festival weekend. People were streaming into town and, even though I'd come in early, all the seats were taken in the chef-demo area in the Market Hall.

The man came and stood slap bang in front of me, blocking my view of the chef's demonstration. I moved to the right. So did he. Then to the left. So did he. Ruddy tourist, I thought. Then someone got up from a seat and I slid into it gratefully. The chef was Italian and not too easy to understand, but the food he was cooking looked wonderful. When the finished dishes were moved to the side table I was ready, out of my seat as quick as you could say Mo Farah and there, spoon in hand, ready to taste the ravioli. As I stretched out my hand another spoon scooped up the succulent little dumpling ahead of me. I turned round, furious and somehow knowing it would be him. I glowered, I hissed, I opened my mouth to swear, but he was gone and when I turned back to the dish, so was the rest of the pasta.

'Delicious, wasn't it?' smiled the woman next to me.

I wanted to tell her she had lipstick on her teeth, but it wasn't true, and anyway it wouldn't have helped. It was the ruddy tourist I was going after. I went and bought a coffee and the stickiest cake I could find. Of a particular type. I sat down, drank the coffee, ate half the cake and thought it through. I definitely knew the town better than he did. I also knew the layout of the Festival better than he would. He was tall and he had red hair. There was no hiding place for him. He was also wearing white trousers. Bad choice Mr Tourist, very bad choice when you mess with Megan Louise Pritchard, resident of Abergavenny.

I thought the chances were that he would head for the cheese and wine area before it got too busy, but there was no sign of him there. I snaffled a couple of cubes of cheese to strengthen my resolve. Round by the Post Office and along to the Castle. Result!—I could see his red hair in front of me. Once inside the Castle grounds I took a back route he wouldn't know. It was ridiculously easy to keep him in view now. I checked my bag. Oh yes, the cake was still there and I was not going to eat it.

I looked at my watch. 12.30. He'd be hungry. He was. I could see that he was tempted by the Thai food wagon, but he was dithering. I didn't mind, he could dither as long as he wanted, hunger would get him in the end and so would I. He walked back and forth and I followed, but he was tall and easy to spot, while I was short and nondescript. For the first time in my life I was glad of this. I was distracted by someone calling my name. It was one of the walking group Susans. I got away from her by saying I was late for a demo and dodged off. The tourist had vanished. How could he vanish?

Then I felt a hand on my shoulder.

'Aren't you the little lady whose ravioli I snatched?' He was smiling. 'Let me buy you some lunch to make up for it?'

I was not going to be deterred. If he wanted to walk right into my trap so be it. I smiled back.

'Thank you', I said, 'You're a gentleman after all.'

'You bag those two spaces then', he said, pointing at one of the trestle tables, 'and I'll get the food.'

I couldn't believe how well this was turning out. Just as he was sitting down I slipped the cake under his buttocks. His white-clad and rather ample buttocks. After lunch, when he stood up to go, the stain from the sticky chocolate was gloriously brown.

He held out his hand: 'Thank you for your company,' he said.

'The pleasure', I replied with total sincerity, 'is all mine.'

All of a muddle

William Evans, the young man who visited Gwladys, told her about the decorations in the Market Hall.

'You should get your daughter to take you down there,' he said. 'It's chickens they've got up there this time. They're amazing.'

'Up there?' she said. 'What d'you mean, up there?'

'Hanging,' he said.

Gwladys was not at all sure that she wanted to see dead chickens strung up in the market hall, it sounded rather gruesome. William had said it was something to do with a Food Festival.

'It was started by some chap who makes ice-cream,' he said.

'Guiseppe? I don't think so,' she said. 'Guiseppe and Lili live in the valleys.'

William had never heard of Gwladys' niece Lili and her Italian husband.

'No, no,' he said. 'I think he's got an English name. You ask your daughter.'

When Megan rang her mum a couple of days later she got a garbled story from her about how William had said that Lili was coming to Abergavenny to sell her husband's ice-cream to chicken farmers, and they had to go to the Market to see her.

'If you'd like an outing we can go to the Market, Mum,' she said, 'But I don't think Lili will be there.'

Stumbles

Such times with Mum. I take her to the Market. There are con trails scrolling in the sky and a breeze on our cheeks. It's early October but summer's not over yet, whatever the doom-mongers say. There's an old man in a good suit and a pork pie hat, hobbling with arthritic knees. And another. I wonder whether they've always dressed up for market, since they were seventeen and their mothers told them it was a day to look tidy.

There are tourists in town, couples in shorts and bare shoulders, browned from the sun of their walking. How lovely, I say to Mum, that they've had some good weather after all that rain, been able to enjoy our hills, eat late wimberries. She says nothing but she turns to me and smiles her old smile and, in that gentle heart-stopping moment, I squeeze her arm.

A couple stop us in the entrance to the Market Hall and ask, the one helping the other out with the English words which stumble in their mouths, if they can drink a coffee somewhere. I laugh because I've counted and there are about forty cafes in the town now. I direct them to a good one, but not to our favourite because we need the quiet of its garden, a haven from the bustle of market day.

Mum stumbles on the steps down to the cafe garden and I support her, stop her from falling. Don't fuss, she says, and I say nothing. There are sunbeams dancing through the trees in the garden haven and I order my favourite coffee and tea for Mum and say we could share a brownie. No, you have a whole one, she says, it might be the last day of summer, spoil yourself Megan.

Afterwards we go into the Market Hall and I point up at the chickens, resplendent in their gold and red silk feathers. I tell Mum I helped to make them and she, for a moment, looks proud. Proud of me, her daughter. Not that she'll ever say, but this moment is precious. I want to wrap it in a scrap of that shining silk and keep it in my box of treasures forever.

But only two weeks later Mum has forgotten that day. When I mention the decorations in the Market Hall she says What decorations? Then I get a phone call from the home care people, who are worried that she's not coping. One of them found a tap running. I say surely anyone could do that, is that all? And of course it isn't all. She needs more help, but I'm not moving in with her. I'm not. Definitely not.

Bronwen

It's only my opinion of course, but I do think Megan should be doing more for her mum. Poor old Gwlad, I do feel so sorry for her, she's my only sister and I do pop in, but I have my Ron to look after, he's had to give up the milk round well you can't go on for ever and his eyesight well, he'd become a danger to himself and there were a couple of little incidents, no-one hurt but some people can be spiteful I find and I don't blame the Company. They gave him a lovely little do actually, it was in the Conservative Club, quite smart, and they presented him with a silver plaque and there was a cake, not as nice a sponge as I could make but never mind, it's the thought, and it had a picture of Ron in his milk float on top, it's amazing the way you can photograph onto icing now I don't know how you do it I'm sure. So there we are.

Christmas is coming, what we'll do I really don't know. We've never had Christmas here, all the family together. But now Glwadys is the way she is she obviously can't have Christmas in that flat and I cannot bear the thought of her being at some old people's Jolly-Them-Along do, half of them dribbling, and doubled-over men with stains on their trouser fronts God help us, if only he could. So, I'll tell Megan to bring her mum over for lunch and no argument. Time was Lili and I used to go over to Gwlad's in that place beginning with B, I don't know, she called it the Home Counties, I always thought that was a funny thing to say, it wasn't her home. Our home when we were kids was in North Wales, different kind of country from round here, but when I met Ron there was no question, he brought me straight down to Abergavenny. He said it was The Place as far as people in the Valleys were concerned. They came here to market and they dreamt of being able to afford to come and live here, love 'em. There's something about that hill, the Blorenge, it's a dark hill, all that history of mining, the coal and the iron, but over on this side, the Valleys people could see that everything was brighter. Which it is, I love Abergavenny, it's been good to me.

Singing for the brain

Singing helps people like Gwladys. Singing for the Brain, they call it. Last bit to go. A group starts up in Abergavenny. There's an announcement about it at coffee after Sunday morning service at St Mary's. A woman Gwladys doesn't recognise tells her she'll pick her up at 10.30 the next day. Gwladys wonders how the woman knows where she lives.

Megan has told her her mum that she should never let strangers into the flat and has written a note to remind her. She's stuck it on the wall by the entryphone. Gwladys sees it when the bell rings.

'It's me, Dorothy. Let me in dear.'

'Who?' says Gwladys.

'Dorothy,' repeats the voice, 'from St Mary's.'

'I'm not going to church today,' says Gwladys.

'No dear, but–'

Gwladys hangs up.

Dorothy rings the bell again, but Gwladys doesn't answer, so Dorothy goes away.

Megan hears about the Singing for the Brain group and tells her mother about it the following week.

'Never heard of it,' says Gwladys.

'That's why I'm telling you now,' says Megan, who had made a resolution when she arrived that morning to be patient with her mother, however many times she asked her the same question. 'I can take you Mum,' she says.

When they get there a woman comes over and greets them.

'You've decided to come this week then,' she says to Gwladys, who looks startled.

'I'm Dorothy dear,' she says. 'From the church.'

Gwladys frowns and turns her back on the would-be-helpful Dorothy, who explains to Megan what had happened, and Megan explains to her just how difficult it is getting with her mother.

Gwladys only goes to Singing for the Brain the once. She doesn't like being jollied along.

'I never did like singing,' she says, and clamps her jaws shut, won't even have a cup of tea.

William's there, the young man who helps at the coffee club. He's training as a carer now. People say he will be good at it, he's done so much for these elderly people. And there are more and more of them who can't manage on their own. As far as he's concerned, it's a job.

Light and dark

When winter comes you only have to live a few miles from town to get cut off because of icy roads on hills. At least that's not going to happen to Mum. And, though I'm not going to move in, definitely not, I go over to see her every day in Christmas week. Lili's back, with Guiseppe and the kids, squeezed in at Bronwen's. I take Mum over there on Christmas Day. Lili cooks the dinner and of course Guiseppe has brought one of his ice-cream cakes. Mum says she's never seen anything like that before, fancy a cake made of ice-cream. Though he'd made one for her 80th, everyone else remembers, even Ron, though he's not the brightest bulb on the Christmas tree these days and nearly sets fire to his hair as he's lighting the sparklers. And we all sit and solemnly watch the Queen's speech and Mum falls asleep and wakes up with a start just as the next inane programme is starting and asks when the Queen will be on. And I wish it was all over and soon it is and then the town and all the people in it are plunged into the dark days of January.

Lili

We all went over to my mum's on the Mardy for Christmas dinner. I got a goose, super-sized 'cos there were going to be so many of us, six adults and the two youngsters. I knew the kids would fill up on chipolatas and that Aunty Gwladys could too. Mum tells me she can be so fussy. In actual fact she was a lamb. I couldn't see then what Mum and Meg were worrying about, she behaved like a normal old lady, a sweetie. She loved the meat, asked for more, and put away at least four roasties. Even ate her sprouts. And asked for a spot more sherry. Bless. She was asleep straight after, not surprising. But not before she'd had the biggest helping of my Beppe's ice-cream cake.

Later Meg and I went upstairs and had a chat like old times. She said she likes Abergavenny. I couldn't wait to get away myself, small-town mentality the people have here. In the Valleys people are more straightforward, don't talk behind your back like I've heard here. I said to Meg that I hope she can cope with the rainy days of winter, her in that cottage near the river too. It can flood quite badly there. And her on her own. She said she's got the cat. Some company, if you ask me. I tried to find out from her whether she's got a boyfriend, but she wasn't telling. Changed the subject. Oh well, maybe she prefers girls, doesn't bother me, each to their own I say.

Fair play, I can see now that things can't be straightforward with Aunty Gwladys. Meg opened up a bit about it as we sat there in my old bedroom, her giving my big old teddy a cwtch, me sitting down on a kiddy's chair and a leg breaking off it. We laughed together, we could always do that, me and Meg. Then she turned serious, said that there's a look on her mum's face sometimes, like she's scared of something but can't tell her what it is. We sat there together for a bit just watching the sun set behind the Deri and the sky streak with pink and purple. A line of starlings smudged across the horizon and a crowd of them descended to their roost in an inky thumb-print.

When it was time to go I said to Meg she should come down, visit me and Beppe and our girls, we'd love to see her any time, and we really would. Family's important to me.

Turn, turn, turn

That January it rains, every day, like the previous summer. I don't go out walking. I still visit Mum once a week, on the day I go into town to go my shopping. I have to wear my wellies, the meadows are so soggy. You can't see the hills for the rain. I sit by the fire with Percy, read melancholy poems and feel sorry for myself. In London I would have been able to go to the theatre, to art galleries. I wonder again why I've chosen a small Welsh town where all that's ever on at the theatre is tribute bands—yes, they have a Beatles one, of course—and not even those in the winter.

Mum's really gone downhill; it upsets me so much. When I go to see her I give her hands a bit of a massage. She's still got a really strong grip. Holding onto life, it feels like. So stubborn, my mum.

One day I'm in town and I bump into Rhodri, the tutor at the Welsh Summer School, my nearly-lover. He asks how my Welsh is and I say it's terrible, I can't even think of the Welsh word for that— 'ofnadwy', he says. But without any reproach.

'Have you got time for coffee?' he says and I say that would be nice, which it is, takes me out of myself. He says he's just visiting a friend; he lives in Cardiff now he does, and I say I'm sorry about that.

'Oh, don't be,' he said, 'Cardiff's a grand place. Why don't you move down there? Abergavenny's such a small town.'

'I can't,' I said. 'My mum—'

'Oh, I'm so sorry,' he said. 'How thoughtless of me. How is she?'

I tell him and it does helps to get it out of my head.

'And. But,' I say. 'I like living here. When Spring comes it's glorious.'

Eventually the grim days of January and February are over. It stops raining. I go out with the women walkers again. There are particular walks, annual pilgrimages, to see the snowdrops, then the early daffodils, the wild Welsh ones, and after that the bluebells.

There's more. Working on those chickens made me realise that I can stitch quite well and I join a group to work on a longer-term project, stitching a landscape in tapestry. Someone's designed the shape of it but we all have a say and we're working on our own sections. I'm stitching a barn, and an owl flying out of it. It's different from the Food Festival workshops, less frenetic. It feeds something in me, a need to express myself that isn't about words. The subtlety of this crafting wraps me up in a kind of restorative cocoon and quietens the voice that nags at me, the voice that says Mum's needs are greater than mine, the voice that tries to make me feel guilty.

The place where we stitch together is up a road I suspect I could never find on my own. It winds round the back of the Sugar Loaf and up into a further valley, to a high farm. At the end of the afternoon, when we set down our work, we walk into the garden to drink our tea and watch the swifts looping as afternoon fades to evening. It's the best of times in the midst of the worst of times.

That final summer the flowers in the garden of my cottage are more abundant and brighter than in any year or any garden I have ever known. I wish Mum could see them, but there's no way I can get her out of her flat now. I take photographs and show her on my laptop, but her eyes glaze. She says she can't see properly.

The time for the Food Festival decorations comes round again. I join in, but I feel slightly removed, as if I'm behind glass. One or two people notice something and ask me if I'm alright but I've gone past talking about it.

The seasons turn. Mum still knows me, but I think she mainly lives in the past. A past before she lived in Abergavenny. A past before she was married and had me. She has such a faraway look in her eyes, and sometimes I see something else and to me it's fear. I can't bear to see her like this, so I don't visit as much as I should do. It feels like it's just a matter of time. Marking time. I honestly don't mean to be cruel. And she has really good care. I was a bit surprised when I saw a man there last week, I mean it's not ideal but we're lucky to get what we do for Mum. Some places you wouldn't get anything like as much and then I'd have to do it and I can't, I just can't. So, I am absolutely not going to make a fuss even though some of the women I walk with say I should, that Mum has a right to have female carers and I should insist. I don't argue with them, I can't win the argument and anyway I am tired of all this and I go out on walks for relief from it all, not to be told I should be complaining to the council. That would just be one more hassle. I just can't. Everyone has their limit.

I recognised him, the carer. He told me his name was William Evans and then I remembered that he was the one from her coffee club who used to visit. He's known her for years, since when she was first in Abergavenny. Then I smiled, because I remember her telling me she'd asked him if he was her long-lost son. I know she liked him. I mean to say, isn't that worth something? He's never going to treat her badly, is he?

Bonfire night

Gwladys edged from the bathroom into her bedroom and lowered herself onto the end of her bed. From there she looked down on the dark of the park. Soon it would be ablaze with lights and from her perch she would have the best view in town of the firework display. Gwladys started, experimentally, swinging her legs. She found, to her surprise, that it was easy. She continued to swing her legs as she watched the people gathering in the park, and something she hadn't felt for a long time started to rise in her. Something that she might have called excitement if there had been anyone there to tell and she could have remembered the word.

Gwladys noticed, as she swung her legs, that there was a length of toilet paper dangling from somewhere. She shrugged and pulled out from the pocket of her apron a packet of sweets which William Evans had given her after she'd refused to eat the cottage pie he'd warmed up for her earlier. As she ripped it open the sweets tumbled out of the packet and onto the carpet. Except for one, which she stuck in her mouth.

William had been Gwladys' five o'clock carer that day. She did not like male carers. She didn't like them seeing 'down there', although all William had done that afternoon was heat up a cottage pie in the microwave and make a cup of tea.

'Nice cup of tea for you, Mrs P,' he'd said in the sing-song way he used to all the old people. 'Going to watch the fireworks tonight, are we?'

Gwladys had said nothing. She was by now stone deaf and refused to wear a hearing aid. She stuck out her chin and puckered her lips obediently as William lifted the cup.

'Drink up,' he said, smiling but tensing the hand which held the cup.

Gwladys slurped the tea, apparently oblivious to his abrupt tone. William glanced over his shoulder at the clock, to see how much time he had before his shift was over and he could go to watch the fireworks like everyone else. His hand jerked and tea dripped down Gwladys' cardigan.

'Now look what you've done!' he shouted at her.

Gwladys leant back in her chair and closed her eyes against the carer and the limitations of old age. William checked that the pie was not so piping hot that it would burn the old lady's mouth and leant towards her with a spoonful. She wrinkled her nose as she smelled it. If she could have thought fast enough and had had the strength, she would have lifted her arm and lobbed the spoonful, indeed the whole dish, off the table. As it was she held her mouth and eyes firmly sealed until she felt a change in the air and knew that the carer must have left the room.

As he shut the door of the flat William hesitated for a moment, because, in his annoyance and rush, he had failed to offer to take Gwladys to the toilet. But he did not turn back; it would have made him late for the fireworks.

Gwladys felt, rather than heard, the slam of her front door. She shuffled in her chair. She was feeling uncomfortable and knew, though she no longer had the words for it, that she needed to go to the toilet. She pressed her hands on the arms of the chair, tensed her shoulders, levered herself onto her feet and began the long slow journey to the bathroom. She did not use her walking frame. Such things, in her opinion, were for namby-pambies. Sometimes she fell. She didn't mind falling, it reminded her of the riding days of her youth, and someone always arrived eventually to pick her up. It was a bit more company, even if they did tell her off. But on this occasion it would have been inconvenient to fall because she did not want to miss the firework display, so Gwladys shuffled along with more care than usual.

Now, having more or less successfully negotiated her trip to the toilet, Gwladys was sucking her sweet. She wondered why William had only left her one. She would have to make it last as long as possible. The taste of it slowly dissolving in her mouth reminded her of the time, she couldn't remember how old she was, when all the

51

children were given marshmallows on sticks; they had turned brown in the fire and tasted like treacle and all the parents had thrown up their hands in horror at the mess.

Down in the park children were whirling sparklers, and the pallets piled up for the bonfire had been set alight. As she watched the flames licking round the feet of the guy, Gwladys recalled a distant time when there had been something that exploded inside a bonfire, and she and all the other children had run around screaming and screaming with delight and fright all mixed up.

Gwladys saw a man in the park look up at her window, smile in a way that was somehow familiar to her and wave. She waved back, wondering where she had seen him before. She had already forgotten that William had told her he was going to the park to see the fireworks. Then she rocked on the edge of her bed and watched the silent explosions of lights over the park, until there was only a misty swirl of half-remembered pictures in her mind and a lingering sweet taste in her mouth.

The magnetism of this place

I don't think Mum was ever actually ill-treated. At least I hope not. But when she died it was a relief. For her and for me. I hated the trap her body had become, her spirit ensnared. When her body was laid in earth, in the cemetery near the river at Llanwenarth, it was not her that we buried. She is with the birdsong and the breeze now. Her spirit is free and can go wherever she wants. That's what I believe. I'm free now, too. To go wherever I will. But I know that I will always return here, and not just to see the spring flowers, amongst them now the snowdrops which we planted on Mum's grave, me and my Aunty Bronwen.

A spider's web is stronger than steel. And so is the pull and hold of Abergavenny. I have made an enduring web of connections here, family and friends dear to me in this little town with its encircling hills, Sugar Loaf, Rholben, Deri, Llanwenarth Breast, Skirrid Fawr, Skirrid Fach and last but not least Blorenge, the only word to rhyme with orange, but not full of water at all. That was only a legend, not the truth. But what those women in the walking group said was true, Abergavenny is a kind of magnet, and it will always draw me back.

Acknowledgements

Sections of the novella previously published:

Revenge is Sweet — in *Abergavenny Focus Magazine* (2012)

Bonfire Night — an earlier version, under the title **Mrs Myfanwy Pritchard**, in *Fictive Dream* (2017)

Biography

Cath Barton's novella **The Plankton Collector** was the winner of the AmeriCymru Prize for the Novella in 2017 and is published by *New Welsh Rarebyte* (2018).

The Geography of the Heart is her fourth published novella, following **In the Sweep of the Bay** (*Louise Walters Books*, 2020) and **Between the Virgin and the Sea** (*Leamington Books*, 2023). Her pamphlet of short stories **Mr Bosch and His Owls** will be published by *Atomic Bohemian* in 2024. She also writes flash fiction and is working on a novel set in the circus.

She lives in Wales and is a keen hill-walker.

The Geography of the Heart is an exceptional collection, and Cath Barton uses the novella-in-flash form to do what could not be accomplished so well in any other form, giving us an insider's look at the way the people in a small town in Wales live. This is an intimate book and a beautiful one too. It is one that I have lingered over a few times now because it asks us to spend some long quiet moments with the inhabitants of Abergavenny, and these are people worth spending time with.

—John Brantingham

Printed in Great Britain
by Amazon